Meet Ella

For Sofya – RM

For Jo, Libby and Lauren – DM

Scholastic Australia
An imprint of Scholastic Australia Pty Limited (ABN 11 000 614 577)
PO Box 579 Gosford NSW 2250
www.scholastic.com.au

Part of the Scholastic Group
Sydney · Auckland · New York · Toronto · London · Mexico City
New Delhi · Hong Kong · Buenos Aires · Puerto Rico

Published by Scholastic Australia in 2022.

NATIONAL LIBRARY OF AUSTRALIA
A catalogue record for this book is available from the National Library of Australia

ISBN: 978-1-76120-429-6

The illustrations in this book were created digitally.
Typeset in KG Neatly Printed and Delius.
Design by Sofya Karmazina.

Printed in China by Hang Tai Printing Company Limited.

This product is made of material from well-managed FSC®-certified forests, recycled materials, and other controlled sources.

FSC www.fsc.org
MIX
Paper | Supporting responsible forestry
FSC® C023121

24 25 26 27 28 / 2

Meet Ella

Lost Book

Rebecca McRitchie ✿ Danielle McDonald

A Scholastic Australia Book

CHAPTER ONE

Meet Ella. She is six years old. Ella likes **bunny rabbits** and **reading books**. Ella doesn't like forgetting things or scrapes on her knees.

Today Ella is in the **library**. She is with her best friend, Zoe. They are looking for books to borrow.

Zoe picks up a green book from the shelf. 'I am going to borrow this one,' she says. 'It's a story about robots.' Zoe makes robot noises with her mouth.
BLEEP. BLOP.

Ella **giggles**.

‘Which book are you going to borrow, Ella?’ Zoe asks.

Ella isn’t sure. She likes two books. One is about a dancing **mermaid**.

The other has a picture of a **bunny** on the cover.

Ella decides to borrow the bunny book. It is called *Funny Bunny*.

Ella and Zoe take their books to Mr Page. Mr Page is the **librarian**. He wears a bow tie.

'I think you will like this one, Ella,' Mr Page says. 'It's very **funny**.'

Mr Page gives Ella and Zoe their books. 'Don't forget to bring these back on Monday,' he says.

When she is outside, Ella throws the *Funny Bunny* book into her bag.

Ella can't wait to read it on the **weekend**!

FUNNY
BUNNY

CHAPTER TWO

The next day is Saturday. Ella wakes up nice and early.

She goes to the **park** with Mum. She helps Dad wash the car. And she plays **dress-ups** in her room.

After lunch, Ella decides to **read** the book from the library. Ella looks inside her school bag. But she can't see the bunny book.

Ella turns her bag upside-down and **shakes** it. Paper, pencils, crayons, and an old apple fall out.

But her book isn't there.

Uh-oh, Ella thinks.

If the book is not inside
her bag, then
where is it?

Ella **searches** everywhere for the *Funny Bunny* book.

She looks under her bed.

And she looks around her stuffed **toys**.

She looks inside the kitchen cupboard.

She looks
under
the couch
cushions.

She looks in the washing
machine.

She looks near the front door. And she even looks in the garbage bins outside!

Oh no!

Ella can't find it anywhere.

She has **lost** her library book. And Mr Page said to bring the book back on Monday.

What is Ella going to do?

CHAPTER THREE

On Sunday night, Ella sits at the table. But she is too **worried** to eat her dinner.

Mum looks at Ella and sees that she has a **frown** on her face. 'What's the matter, Ella?' Mum asks. 'You haven't touched your carrots.'

'I've lost my book,' Ella says quietly.

'The one from the school library?' Dad asks.

Ella nods. 'It's due **tomorrow**. And I didn't even get to read it!' Now she will never know what happens to the funny bunny.

'Maybe Olivia can help you look for it?' Mum says.

Olivia is Ella's younger **sister**. She is three years old. Olivia claps her hands. She is **excited** to help Ella.

'We can be detectives!' Ella says.

Ella and Olivia go to the dress-up box. Ella uses a **magnifying glass** like a detective. Maybe it will help her find the book. Olivia wears a detective hat.

Together, Ella and Olivia **look** under the couch.

'Found it!' says Olivia. But it is just the remote control.

They look under Olivia's bed.

‘Found it!’ says Olivia. But it is just her stuffed teddy, George.

They look and look and find lots of lost things. But none of them are Ella's **lost book**.

'What if it's lost forever?' Ella says.

'I'm sure it will turn up,' says Dad.

'If not, Mr Page will understand,' says Mum.

Before bed, Ella searches her room again. Where could her book be? What is she going to say to Mr Page? Will she be able to **borrow** books again?

CHAPTER FOUR

At school, Zoe finds Ella.

'Did you like your book, Ella? Mine had so many **robots** in it!' Zoe says.

'I didn't get to read it,' says Ella. 'I lost it.'

Zoe gasps.

'Can you help me look for it?' Ella says.

In class, Ella and Zoe **search** their desks. The *Funny Bunny* book isn't there.

And at lunch, Zoe and Ella search the **playground**.

Ella's tummy flips and flops. What is she going to say to Mr Page?

'Hi, Ella and Zoe,' someone says.

It is Alexander. His shirt has crumbs on it from his lunch.

'Are you looking for this?' Alexander asks. He holds out a book to Ella.

It is *Funny Bunny*!

'Thank you, Alexander,' Ella says. 'Where was it?'

'I found it **outside** the library,' Alexander says. 'And I heard you looking for it.'

Outside the library! It must have **fallen** from her bag.

'It looks really **funny**,' Alexander says. 'I might borrow it after you.'

Ella is so **happy** the *Funny Bunny* book has been found. Her stomach stops flipping and flopping.

Now Ella can take the book back to the library!

CHAPTER FIVE

Ella and Zoe find Mr Page in the **library**. Zoe gives Mr Page her robot book. And Ella hands him the *Funny Bunny* book.

‘Thanks for returning these on time,’ Mr Page says. ‘Did you like the story of the funny bunny, Ella?’

'I don't know,' Ella says. 'I didn't get to read it.'

'Oh, why not?' asks Mr Page.

Ella isn't sure what to say. 'I thought I took it home but I **dropped** it outside.'

Mr Page **smiles**. Then he gives the book back to Ella.

'You can bring it back tomorrow,' says Mr Page.

'Really?' Ella says.

Mr Page nods.

Ella is so happy. She gets to read *Funny Bunny*! This time, Ella **carefully** opens up her bag and puts the book inside.

She zips up her bag tightly.

That night, Ella finds the *Funny Bunny* book. She reads it before bed. And Mr Page is right! It is really **funny**. She can't wait to tell Zoe all about it.

And guess what? There's a **second** *Funny Bunny* book! Ella is going to read it next.

Ella **loves** borrowing books from the library!

If you loved *Meet Ella*, join her for more adventures!